hello airplane!

airplane!

Written and illustrated by
Bill Cotter

sourcebooks
jabberwocky

Mixed media were used to prepare the full color art.

Published by Sourcebooks Jabberwocky, an imprint of Sourcebooks, Inc.
P.O. Box 4410, Naperville, Illinois 60567-4410
(630) 961-3900
Fax: (630) 961-2168
www.jabberwockykids.com
Library of Congress Cataloging-in-Publication data is on file with the publisher.

Source of Production: Leo Paper, Heshan City, Guangdong Province, China
Date of Production: August 2014
Run Number: 5001929
Printed and bound in China.
LEO 10 9 8 7 6 5 4 3 2 1

To Brady, Kelci, and Tripp.

The airplane says
good-bye to the ground.

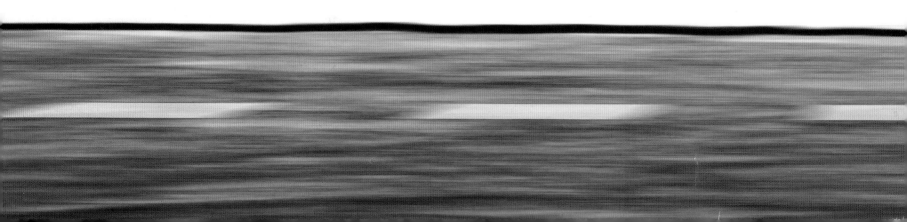

The airplane says hello to the sky.

The airplane is filled with people.

The airplane flies over the town.

The airplane flies over the trees.

The airplane flies over the mountains.

The airplane flies through the clouds.

The airplane flies through the night.

The airplane says hello to the stars.

The airplane flies into the morning.

**The airplane makes
shadows on the clouds.**

The **airplane** **flies above the** **birds.**

The airplane flies over the people.

The airplane says hello to the ground.

Good-bye, airplane!